To Pippin who popped off

To Simba who popped in

HERTFORDSHIRE COUNTY COUNCIL

ST. PETER'S COUNTY PRIMARY SCHOOL

OLD LONDON ROAD
ST. ALBANS.

Headmaster: P. G. GOULD
Telephone: St. Albans 53075

8th March, 1963.

Dear Mr. Piggopotamus, I regret that there has been difficulty regarding
Clive's clothing. Naturally I have asked the teacher to arrange
stricter control of changing arrangements so that clothes are now
left on the pupil's desk.

With so many children wearing the same kind of grey sweater I
notice that many of them now have name tabs sewn inside. I understand
Clive now has his own garment.

Unfortunately, Clive has been more careless than most of his class-
mates and his teacher has had to retrieve articles from many odd
corners where he had thrown them. Several children claim that he
lost his plimsole outside school and certainly a most thorough
search has proved unsuccessful. We haven't lost a plimsole in
school for some time although they are frequently mislaid for a
day or so.

Yours sincerely,

P. G. Gould

JURASSIC COVE
& OTHER JOLLY JAPES

by

Clive PiG

with illustrations by
Andrew Kingham

Published in Great Britain in 2016 by Caboodle Books Ltd.

Copyright © 2016 Clive PiG

Design and illustrations by Andrew Kingham.

Photograph on back cover by Harry Duns.

Typeset in Century Schoolbook, Burnstown Dam and Providence.

A Catalogue record for this book is available from the British Library.

ISBN: 978-0-9933000-8-0

Printed and bound by CPI Group (UK) Ltd, Croydon, CR0 4YY

The paper and board used in the paperback by Caboodle Books Ltd. are natural recyclable products made from wood grown in sustainable forests. The manufacturing processes conform to the environmental regulations of the country of origin.

Caboodle Books Ltd.

Riversdale, 8 Rivock Avenue,

Steeton, BD20 6SA UK.

Tel: +44 (0)1535 656015

www.authorsabroad.com

Dear Reader,

Whoever and wherever you are at this moment, I am very, very chuffed that you're holding this book in your hands.

Perhaps you purchased it from me personally at one of my many gigs where you'll have seen and heard me perform some of these poems and stories already. Perhaps you bought it from a book shop or by way of the internet. You might have borrowed it from a library, been given it as a present or even found it by chance – as I have a tendency to leave copies in random places.

Whichever of the above, I hope you enjoy my wordy ways and the inedible illustrations of my long time collaborator and conspirator, Andrew Kingham. I'd also like to thank Sophie Mortimer for roof preading lis manuskrypt.

It took me 57 years to produce my first book *PiG's Tales,* and at that rate my second book was scheduled for the year 2071. I hope you're glad you didn't have to wait that long.

Toodle-pip!

CONTENTS

THAT WAY

As Many Stars As Stories

At the end of the story
She threw another log on the campfire
And showers of sparks fizzed.
Some steamed the wet grass,
Some landed in our hot chocolate.
One singed my sock.

Others dashed upwards –
Tiny sparkles tickling
Flickering faces beneath dark trees.
We watched these baby stars
Swirling through the smoke
Dart towards the Milky Way.

The storyteller leaned forwards
And as she spoke
Showers of words fizzed from her mouth,
'There are as many tales down here
As there are stars up there.'

And she began another story ...

Planet Birth

Those who came before us made our world.
But it is not finished nor will it ever be.

We walk upon our grandfather's skull
                    and his teeth are the mountains.
But it is not finished nor will it ever be.

Grandmother danced and her footprints are stars.
But it is not finished nor will it ever be.

The sun and the moon are our father's eyes.
But it is not finished nor will it ever be.

Our mother's hair became the plants and her
                    blood is the rivers and seas.
But it is not finished nor will it ever be.

Her fleas became fish and all the creatures of
                        the world.
But it is not finished nor will it ever be.

Our first brothers and sisters were made from mud.
But it is not finished nor will it ever be.

They had no thoughts and were drowned
                      in the flood.
But it is not finished nor will it ever be.

Others were then made out of wood.
But it is not finished nor will it ever be.

They were not grateful so burned in the fire.
But it is not finished nor will it ever be.

Trees rose from the ashes and burst into blossom.
But it is not finished nor will it ever be.

Bees kissed the flowers and we were the fruits.
But it is not finished nor will it ever be.

And when we were ripe we fell to the ground.
But it is not finished nor will it ever be.

You are our children and you will have children.
But it is not finished nor will it ever be.

Tell them – those who came before us made
our world.
But it is not finished nor will it ever be.

New Word

There is a word
That has never been said.

Never been written,
Never been read.

Never been whispered,
Shouted or sung.

Never been uttered or muttered
Or stuttered or spluttered

But now it has sprouted,
Now it's begun,

It's about to be spouted,
Look out, here it comes
Off the tip of the tongue

And that word is...

Len Lent A Pen

Len lent a pen to Ben
Who lent the pen to Ken
Who lent the pen to Gwen
Who lent the pen to Chen.

Chen then lent the pen to Vivienne
Who then lent it to Fen.
Fen then lent the pen to Etienne
Who then lent it to Sven.

Sven then thought of Len
So passed it back to Etienne
Who gave the pen to Fen.
Fen gave it then to Vivienne

Who gave the pen to her friend Chen.
Chen passed it on to his friend Gwen
Who gave it back to her friend Ken.
Ken passed the pen to his friend Ben

Who gave it back to his friend Len.

And what do you think?
It had run out of ink.

Len never lent a pen again.

Mrs winterbottom and the Gingerbread Man

I always try and tailor my material for the varied audiences I encounter but sometimes I just get it wrong.

Once, when telling a traditional tale in an assembly at an Infant school in the UK, I noticed that, as the story unfolded, someone at the back was becoming more and more distressed. The longer I spoke the worse it became.

At the beginning I'd heard a sharp intake of breath; towards the middle, gasps and moans; and as I was reaching the climax, sniffling, wailing and then force 10 gale blubbering.

The Deputy Head had to escort someone from the hall and then everyone looked at me as if I'd drowned three kittens in a bucket of water.

I said I was really sorry and embarrassed, but I'd told that story many times before, even at mother and toddler groups, and it had never had that reaction.

I didn't know what else to say.

Once the hall had emptied in silence the Deputy Head returned and said the Head Teacher wanted to see me in her office.

Uh oh, I thought, I'll never work in this school again.

I knocked on the door and Mrs Winterbottom opened it and said,

'Clive, can I borrow your handkerchief? I've run out of tissues.'

Of course I could. I lent her one of my red and white spotted ones.

After she'd dried her eyes and wrung out my hanky over the pot plant, she told me she'd always found that story upsetting and couldn't I give it a happy ending to make her feel better?

I wondered if that's the sort of thing story-tellers were supposed to do.

She replied that, once upon a time, Goldilocks was an old woman and her name had been Silverhair.

Well, I thought, if that's the case I can give it a go but I might have to change some other parts of the story too.

She said I had her permission.

And so, making sure she was sitting comfort-ably, the following words popped out of my mouth ...

Once upon a time when pigs could fly and beards could talk, there was an old man and an old woman who lived in a cottage at the end of the lane.

All of their children had grown up. They'd become so tall their heads bumped against the ceiling and they'd all left home.

One of them had gone to America. One had gone to Australia. One had gone to Antarctica. And the other seven had gone to live in the alley with Aunty Sally.

One day the old woman said to her husband, 'I do miss the sound of them stomping around the place and shouting and cursing every time their heads smashed the light bulbs. I'd like to have another child. I want to take it to the park and watch it play on the swings until it falls off and grazes its kneezes and I'll rush over and I'll hug it and kiss it and make everything as right as rain again.'

Her husband was not very pleased with that and replied,

'Well don't look at me. I'm too old for that sort of thing. I don't want anything to do with it. I've got enough on my plate, what with painting the pond and cutting the grass with a pair of scissors.'

'Don't worry your bonce about that,' laughed the wife. 'I'll make a child just for me. A child that won't grow up and leave home like the others.'

She went to the cupboard and brought out all the ingredients. She mixed them together in a bowl, kneaded the dough and then rolled it out on the kitchen table. She took a wooden knife and cut out a head, arms, tummy and legs. She poked a belly button with her little finger.

The old woman sang a song with no words while she gave him two currants for eyes. She whistled a silent tune and gave him a wild strawberry nose. She hummed like a bumble bee and made him a smiley mouth of cherry jam.

She dressed him in a jacket of marzipan with three chocolate buttons. She covered his legs with butter cream icing. She wondered about buying him some trainers but decided they were too expensive.

She looked down at her little creation and said to it,

'My, you're a crafty work of art. I'm very proud of you. You're a beauty that's for sure. But listen to me, you little fellow. I don't want you turning out like the others, running off and leaving me. I want us to stay together forever and ever.'

It wasn't worth wasting fuel heating up the big oven for such a little thing, so she scooped him up with a spatula and put him in the microwave. Thirty seconds later the pinger pinged and she opened up the glass door and out span a little biscuit boy.

WheeeeeeeeeeEEEEEEEEEEEEEEEE!

He span off the four walls, bounced off the ceiling and landed on the floor. He shook his head, he rubbed his arms and felt to see if his legs were broken.

'Cripes and crumbs!' said the little fellow.

'Hello', said the old lady, 'look at you. My own little Gingerbread Boy.'

Well, he didn't like the sound of that at all. He stood up, puffed out his chest and said in a shrill voice that shattered the windows, 'I'm a man. I'm not a boy.' And with that he dashed through the cat flap and darted down the lane singing,

'Run, run as fast as you can,
You can't catch me,
I'm the Gingerbread Man.'

'Oh dear,' wailed the old woman, 'too many additives in the flour or too much zing in the ginger?'

She hobbled out of the cottage as fast as she could to catch him but tripped over a tortoise and fell into the pond.

By and by, the Gingerbread Man came to a field. George Clooney, Brad Pitt and Bradley Wiggins were bare to the waist, muscles rippling and dripping with perspiration, cutting golden wheat with bronze sickles sparkling in the sunlight.

(This is Mrs Winterbottom's fantasy, not mine.)

They looked up to see the biscuit boy passing by and invited him to come over and have a word or two. But the Gingerbread Man wasn't having any of that.

'I don't like the look of you three,' he said in a shrill voice that made the birds fly to the moon. 'I know what you want to do. You want to chop me in three with those big curved knives. Well, I've run away from the old woman and now I'll run away from you.'

And with that he ran along the way singing,

'Run, run as fast as you can,
You can't catch me,
I'm the Gingerbread Man.'

By and by, the Gingerbread Man came to a tree where there was a woman with ten fingers and two thumbs standing on a branch picking potatoes. As he paused for breath she invited him to climb up and sing her a song while she had her elevenses.

But the biscuit boy shook his head and said in a shrill voice that made the potatoes fall from the tree and bury their heads in the ground,

'I know what you want to do. You want to dunk me in your mug of milky coffee and gobble me up. Well, I'm not having that. I've run away from the old woman, I've run away from those three muscly men Mrs Winterbottom fancies, and now I'll run away from you.'

And that's just what he did, singing,
'Run, run as fast as you can,
You can't catch me,
I'm the Gingerbread Man.'

By and by, the Gingerbread Man came to a tree full of people with open books and blank pages holding pens and looking pensive. Can you guess what sort of tree it was? Yes, you've got it. It was a Poet Tree. And the poets called to him and asked if they could paint a picture of him with words.

But the biscuit boy shook his head and said in such a shrill voice that the books burst into flames,

'No, you can't paint a picture of me with words. There aren't enough letters in the alphabet to do me justice. There aren't the right words in the dictionary to describe the complexity of my personality. The only writer who could get half way close is William Shakespeare and he's dead.'

Well, that made the poets really angry and they jumped down from the tree and tried to crush him to crumbs but the little fellow screeched in a voice that made the sun cover its ears,

'I've run away from the old woman, I've run away from three muscly men, I've run away from that woman with two extra fingers and now I'll run away from you.'

And with that he shot off singing,

'Run, run as fast as you can,
You can't catch me,
I'm the Gingerbread Man.'

By and by, the Gingerbread Man came to a

lake. To the right there was a hippopotamus rolling in some mud. To the left there was a crocodile pretending to be a log. But straight in front of him there was an old red fox. And the fox called out,

'Quick, little Gingerbread Man. Climb on to my back. Everyone's after you, but I can take you to safety. I'll give you a ride to the other side.'

The Gingerbread Man looked behind and saw all the people running towards him. He turned one way and saw the hippo licking its lips. He turned the other way and saw the crocodile pretending to be a log gnashing its jaws.

He turned to the fox and looked straight into his red and black zigzag eyes and asked,

'Can I trust you? Can I really trust you?'

'There's no time for questions,' snapped the fox, 'get on board quick.'

He swished his tail and the Gingerbread Man was whisked onto the fox's furry back as the crocodile and the hippo plodded towards them. The fox leapt into the lake and they were almost a quarter of the way across when the two belligerent beasts slunk into the water. Half way across, the fox panted,

'You're weighing me down. Climb on to my head and hold on tight.'

Three quarters of the way across the fox warned,

'I'm running out of strength. I don't think I'll make it to the other side.'

The Gingerbread Man looked behind and saw the wickedest smile on the crocodile and the hippo's cave of a mouth surging towards them as fast as a tidal wave. The fox's head was sinking lower into the water and the biscuit boy's little feet were getting soggy.

The fox gasped,

'Hurry, little fella. They're closing in on us. Climb onto my nose. It's your only hope.'

And so he climbed up onto the fox's nose.

(At this point Mrs Winterbottom almost fainted.)

A split second before the croc and the hippo snapped their jaws shut, the fox tossed the Gingerbread Man into the air and the little biscuit boy was caught by a friendly gust of wind and blown like a leaf to the other side of the lake.

As he drifted down below he saw many merry mermaids riding bicycles, three horned unicorns galloping around a castle and lots and lots of pretty princesses dressed in black playing in the skate park.

And there he stayed and there he played and there he lived happily ever after. But please don't ask me what happened to the old red fox. I think you can guess, so there's no need to spell it out is there?

Now, if you liked this tale
Or if you liked it not.
It's time to end this story
With a big full STOP

Weather (or Not?)

Severe weather warning issued by the Vet Office.

Early risers in the south will need tough umbrellas, as it will be raining cats and dogs first thing tomorrow.

If you live at the opposite end of the country, have a torch handy as there will be thick frog.

You'll need your wits about you in the west, particularly drivers in Cornwall, as we're expecting severe lizards on Bodmin Moor.

In the east there'll be a frosty start, so watch your step as there'll be lots and lots of slippery mice.

And I'm afraid all's not boding well for those staying at home living in poorly insulated houses, as there could well be lots of giraffes coming under the door, through cracked windows and down the chimney.

Wherever you are tomorrow be prepared for the unexpected. The weather will be behaving in a curious manner.

Flora's Flip-Flops

Flora's flip-flops were a flop
Stock in beach shop not tip top

Skiddy, no grippy
The pier was so slippy

She flop-flipped into sea
She could not stop.

Seaside Swag

I love to sift sand in my hand,
These little bits of what was land.

Hey, leave that stone alone!
It's my stone,
I want to take it home.

And that shell as well.

And I need that seaweed.

That driftwood's very good.

I'll put them in my carrier bag,
My swell selection of seaside swag.

I wish I could take the whoosh of the waves,
I'll photograph the cliffs and caves
To remind me of my holiday
When winter days are cold and grey.

I'd take the whole beach if I could,
Especially the rock pools.

But I can't take home what I really wish,
Dad won't let me take the dead dogfish.

He took it out the car boot,
I thought I'd hidden it quite well.
I'd wrapped in a beach towel,
But he found it by the smell.

I was going to keep it in my bedroom
And put it on the shelf
Next to my lump of elephant poo.

Jurassic Cove

The first day of the summer holidays was as bright and full of endless possibilities as were Oscar and George. These two bestest of friends whooped in delight as they bundled into the back of the car and played I Spy all the way to the beach.

The sky was as blue as Oscar's eyes and the seaweed as green as George's face last July when he rode the roller coaster after eating a Knickerbocker Glory.

They plonked bags and towels on the dry sand by the rocks and stood gobbling bananas, eyeballing the cove.

Their mums had something terribly, terribly important to talk about which suited the boys just fine. They snuck off to the cliff, ignored the danger signs and disappeared into the narrow slit of a cave.

Oscar cursed like a pirate. George laughed like an ogre. Rowdy echoes bounced back promising a proper cave. Torch beams picked out a dead cormorant, a buckled fishing rod and dozens of plastic bottles. They didn't know what they were looking for but would know when they found it.

As the walls widened, George pushed by, eager to be the first to find some seaside swag. Oscar reached down and picked up a stone with a hole in it and shoved it in his pocket. George found a decent piece of amber but then groaned. The cave had ended. They'd have to go back.

George always gave up first. Oscar would show him. He grabbed a dinosaur bone, thrust one end under an armpit and hopped about like a one-legged sea dog singing a sea shanty. Not to be outdone, George became the Dorset Ooser* dancing manically as Oscar flicked his torch off and on in the darkness.

After tiring of this they were about to head back when they heard mumblings and mutterings coming from behind the far wall.

Pretending to be a miner digging for minerals, Oscar hacked at the rock face with his bone. As soon as the bone touched the wall he felt a shock, he saw a flash and the wall collapsed. When the dust settled the friends spied a strange old woman huddled over a steaming cauldron in a green, glowing grotto.

Dorset Ooser ... A legendary horned giant.

She was a jumble of flotsam and jetsam. Her head was a marker buoy crowned with an inflatable rubber ring. A peeling eyepatch made of car tyre was half stuck on her orange face and her one good eye seemed to be a sea anemone. Water dripped from her whelk-shell nose into her pouty fishy mouth and then dribbled into a tuft of seaweed stuck on her chin. She wore a shawl of sail cloth with sandflies hopping about her shoulders.

Her arms and legs were pieces of driftwood dotted with barnacles poking out of a lobster pot. Her fingers and toes were fishhooks and feathers. A tangle of nylon fishing net entwined with blue rope seemed to hold the whole kit and caboodle together.

Stirring the cauldron with a dinghy paddle, she spoke with a voice that sounded like the creaking timbers of a galleon.

'This potion's bubbling nice and hot,
But something's missing from my pot.
A dino's bone for my brew.
Is that one there?
Give it here, you two!'

She snatched it out of Oscar's hand and chucked it into the cauldron.

The two boys stared at the curious creature and then at the green steam rising from the bubbling concoction. The sea witch tasted the broth then spat it back into the pot through her teeth of rusty rivets. She cracked a seagull's egg on the side of the pot, stirred it in and finally scooped up a handful of sand to thicken the soup. The hag then plunged a drowned sailor's skull into the brew and offered it to the boys.

Oscar looked at George, George looked at Oscar: 'Me first!' each cried.

Together they grabbed the hollow head, guzzled the salty brine, drained the last drop and instantly felt a strange tingling sensation rising from the pits of their stomachs to the tops of their heads, from the tips of their fingers to the tips of their toes.

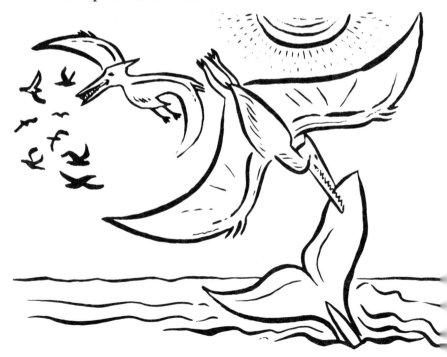

Their bones shook. Their skin crackled. Their veins bulged. Their heads span.

The next they knew they were flying side by side in the cloudless sky. Their mothers, oblivious to what was going on above their heads were still having their terribly, terribly important conversation.

But everyone else at the seaside was pointing up to the sky. The boys tried to wave back but it's very hard to wave when your arms have become wings, and it's very hard to smile when you've got a long beak.

For the next sixty minutes a pair of pterodactyls shocked and thrilled holiday makers and locals alike.

To rapturous applause the flying reptiles terrorised the ice cream-snaffling, chip-splattering seagulls, clearing the startled scavengers from the cove. Then, to the delight of the crowd below, they performed an aerial display much more daring than the Red Arrows before dive-bombing a great white shark lurking in the bay about to sink its teeth into the pink and yellow lilo on which lay the well loved local celebrity, Penelope Picklemonger.

As the shark skulked away, the pterodactyls rose up into the heavens with cheers ringing in their ears. They were about to set off on a race around the planet when without warning each wingbeat became slower and their bodies heavier and heavier.

Instead of speeding up, the two friends began to falter.

Sadly, their aerial antics were over. With their powers waning, it was all they could do to steady their nerves and steer a course to glide safely back into the cave in the cove.

They tumbled into the cavern and begged the sea hag for more of the magical salty brew. She stared at George with her one anemone eye and spoke with a voice that sounded like heavy waves crashing against a cliff on a stormy night.

'This potion's bubbling nice and hot,
But something's missing from my pot.
If I don't get it,
That's your lot.
Give me a gander at your amber.'

As soon as George showed it to her, the sea

hag snatched it and tossed it into the pot. A second later the boys drank greedily from the skull.

Once more they felt a strange sensation rising from the pits of their stomachs to the tops of their heads, from the tips of their fingers to the tips of their toes.

Their bones shook. Their skin crackled. Their veins bulged. Their heads span.

They emerged from the cave and plodded past their mums who were still having their terribly, terribly important conversation. All the others on the beach watched in stilled silence as a

couple of dark grey dinosaurs lumbered towards the sea. Those close by hurriedly moved their beach paraphernalia out of the way but nothing could be done to save their sandcastles.

Once Oscar and George were buoyant out in the bay the dinosaur duo bowed their long necks and with booming bellows beckoned to all and sundry to climb aboard.

Hundreds of people hollered with joy and splashed into the sea.

The two friends entwined their necks to make a giant helter skelter. After three goes each, everyone climbed aboard and had a fabulous tour around the bay.

But once again, almost an hour later, the magic began to wear off. It was all the pair could do to get their passengers safely to the shore. Lobsters and crabs dropped from their dripping, ailing hulks onto the sand. As the brontosauruses, each heavy as an oil rig, trudged wearily towards the cave, the smell of barbecued seafood wafted into their frisbee-sized nostrils.

Stumbling into the cavern they begged the sea hag for more of the magical salty brew. A hermit crab scuttled around her neck and disappeared behind a cuttlefish ear. She stared at Oscar with her anemone eye and roared like the Kraken,

'This potion's bubbling nice and hot,
But something's missing from my pot.
A special stone should do the trick,
It's in your pocket,
Give it! Quick!'

Oscar dug into his pocket then plopped the stone with a hole into the pot. Seconds later, the pals drank keenly from the skull.

Once more they felt a strange sensation rising from the pits of their stomachs to the tops of their heads, from the tips of their fingers to the tips of their toes.

Their bones shook. Their skin crackled. Their veins bulged. Their heads span.

It had already been a very special day for most of the people at Jurassic Cove. After all, it's not every day that you see a pterodactyl or a brontosaurus, let alone a pair of each. But many later agreed that the highlight had been watching a couple of Tyrannosaurus Rexes playing beach

football with an ice cream van. Years later when grown men and women recounted being given a piggyback by a dinosaur, listeners would shake their heads in wonder. Children would remember forever and ever the day they played in a life-size sandcastle made by two of the friendliest T.Rexes you'd ever hope to meet.

Unfortunately, all of this excitement was missed by two mothers on the beach who'd been having their terribly, terribly important conversation right up until mid-afternoon when they realised they hadn't seen their sons for the best part of the day.

Suddenly they jumped up and looked around. One ran to the sea, one ran to the cliff. They called out the boys' names. They dashed back in panic about to ring emergency services when a woman lying on a towel nearby said,

'Don't worry dears. They've been having a wonderful time rushing in and out of that cave. Such lively imaginations. I wish my boys were like that. I can't get mine off their phones.'

At that moment, Oscar and George appeared and cried,

'Can we have our picnic now? We're starving!'

Not Chuffed

I hiked to the cliffs on the Cornish coast
Where ancient tin mines be.
To spot the bird that Kernow boasts,
On its coat of arms stands he.
This charming crow's red legs and beak
Are famed in Cornish lore.
My aim? A peek of which drolls' speak
As I clambered down to the shore.

I waited and waited as still as a rock
Beneath a granite grey sky.
I got cramp in the damp as I sat in a squat,
Not one single chough did I spy.
They'd said they were special,

      I'd read they were rare,
But I'm sure they no longer exist.
For I went for a gander and they were not there,
Your tourist board's taking the ... mick.

True, I heard the whoop of The Hooper,
Coming from mist in the bay.
I saw the ghost of a wrecker,
Loading his spoil on a dray.

A tinner trudged by with a pasty
And following close behind –
A knocker, a bucca, a spriggan, a piskie?
An imp of some very odd kind.

Giants hurled rocks at each other,
The Beast of Bodmin yowled.
But *they* weren't why I'd gone to this bother,
I arose to complain and I scowled.
Mermaids and selkies frolicked galore,
Pirates swashbuckled and swore.
Cliffs shook to the roar of the serpent Morgawr,
But really what was the last straw

Was The Owlman of Mawnan appearing at dusk,
He flew above me with a hoot.
When I saw his sharp talons I knew that I must
Exit now – it was time to scoot.
Up sprang a dancing, standing stone,
Getting past was such a palaver.
And guess who I met on his horse heading home?
You're right – it was blooming King Arthur!

When I returned to my tent on the campsite,
Faeries fiddled and pranced on the Gump*.
No sleep did I get through that long

raucous night

And by dawn I was left with the hump.

So all you good people, I think you should know,
All us grockles* have been hoodwinked.
Don't go on a quest for the Cornish crow –
The blinking bird's extinct.

* *The Gump ... A hill in West Cornwall where pixies hold their revels.*
* *Grockles ... Cheeky Cornish term for tourists.*

There Was A Young Man From Ashburton

There was a young man from Ashburton,
Who tore down and ripped up a curtain.
He swore and he screamed
At his sewing machine
Now he strides through the town with a skirt on.

Anton Often Wondered ...

Anton often wondered how long the goldfish would survive if he swallowed it.

He wasn't squeamish about such matters as he was the sort of boy who could scoff fifty Brussels sprouts – raw. He'd won the school's prune eating competition twice. And once he'd downed a litre of Anastasia's Apocalyptic Concoction without being sick for almost half an hour.

Besides, he'd be doing the little creature a favour. It would have much more fun swimming in his tummy for a while rather than around and around a big glass bubble forever.

He wasn't worried about his parents finding out. They were too busy to notice such trifling matters. His sister would be the problem as she was quite attachcd to it. But he could deal with her.

Anyway, if the goldfish didn't die he could always fish it out later and put it back in the bowl. That would confuse Clarissa.

Carefully he lowered the small green net into the water and scooped the goldfish out. It wriggled and splashed water on to the table.

For a few split seconds he watched the glittering creature gasping for life and then he lifted it to his face, opened his mouth and slapped the back of the net so that the flickering fish shot onto his tongue and slid down his throat like a kid on a water chute.

Wheeee! Down it shot into his stomach.

It tickled a bit but not much. It was only a little fish. Nothing to make a fuss about. It wasn't the size of that salmon he'd seen in the river last autumn. He wouldn't have been able to swallow that in one go.

Hurriedly he wiped the table, then dried the net on a tea towel and put it away in the drawer.

The bowl seemed lonely now that nothing was moving around inside. He thought about emptying it and then putting it on his head and being an astronaut for the rest of the afternoon.

Still, as it was, he had enough to occupy him. He wondered if the goldfish might glow in the dark. Then he thought that he should have probably swallowed a tropical fish as it might be too warm inside his tummy for a cold water fish. If only the goldfish could contact him to give him a clue about what was going on.

Anton was beginning to realise he hadn't planned this experiment properly.

Suddenly his insides began to throb. He held his stomach and it was moving like when

Clarissa was in Mum's tum.

Then it all went still.

Anton had forgotten all about the baby grass snake he'd swallowed last summer.

The idea of a reptile growing inside him turned his stomach. He rushed into the garden and picked up a frog from the pond. Dangling it upside down at arm's length, he opened his mouth and waited for the snake to rise to the bait.

An hour later he felt the grass snake stirring in his belly and glide up his throat until its head was looking out of his mouth. Its tongue flickered and then it shot forward and swallowed the frog whole.

Anton quickly snapped his mouth shut and bit off the end of the snake's tail. He spat it out as the wounded snake dropped to the lawn and slithered off into the compost heap.

After wiping his mouth he looked at his watch and seeing it was only 3 o'clock found himself at a loose end. But then Anton remembered the goldfish bowl and wondered whether it would fit easily or would he have to rub some butter on it to slip it over his head?

Anton went back into the house to find out.

Caroline's Not Fine

Caroline!
Fine is not fine,
It makes me prickly as a porcupine.

There will be a fine, Caroline,
If you think, write or say *fine*, Caroline.

Fine is like a grape that has withered on
the vine.

It has no spine,
It does not shine,
It's anodyne,
It is supine,
It must resign,
Consign it to that black bin of mine.

It should not be at the beginning, the middle or the end of the line.

In my book it's a crime, Caroline.
Please do not opine, Caroline.

If you use that awful word one more time, Caroline.

You'll have to write out *cryptocrystalline*, Caroline.

100 times, Caroline.
On blank paper in straight lines, Caroline.

Do you understand me, Caroline?

Fine is not fine!

The Hole In The Wall Gang

'Felix, guess what? More weirdness. We were waiting at the bus stop by Cathedral Alley when a dog goes ballistic. Over the road, a couple of chavs were giving a Big Issue girl a hard time. Before I could stop her, Mum dashed across the road and started giving the kids a mouthful. It was *sooo* embarrassing! Then our bus came round the corner. I called to her, but she wasn't bothered. Everyone else got on and it drove off. Typical!

'You know what Mum's like. She's got a lot of bottle. "Stand up for what you believe in." She's always saying that. But it's all right for her. She's not scared of anything.

'So, I look over and the chavs have gone, and she's hanging out with Homeless. Oh no, I think, we'll be sleeping in the garden shed and her new friend and her mates'll be dossing in our rooms.

'But no, it was OK. She just bought a magazine and came back over. At least now we were first in the queue. She started going on about the chavs, and how much they'd looked like trolls. Then I saw three little hoodies come out from a hole in a wall. Yes, from the cash dispenser of the bank!

'They were titchy, much smaller than me. In their mitts they had loads of paper notes. I thought, 'What! Toddlers on a bank raid? Hilarious!'

'I looked around for their getaway pedal car, but they didn't seem to be in much of a hurry. They walked into the crowd and then they spread out in a line, like those annoying leaflet hander-outers. What were they going to do now? I wondered. Trip everyone over, nut them in the privates?

'I could see they were looking for likely

candidates. One of them pointed out an old woman pulling a wheelie basket behind her. They waited for her to get close and then stuffed a £20 note into her coat pocket. Another one pushed a tenner into the hand of a baby in a pushchair.

'I heard Mum say, "Staring into thin air again?" But I couldn't help it. I knew she wouldn't be able to see what was going on and I wasn't going to go tell her our new secret.

'I turned to her just to say something to keep her quiet but she was texting, so I went back to watching the great Lilliputian lottery bonanza.

'They were scurrying about, placing a fifty here, plugging a twenty there. They only targeted those who looked like they could really do with it. When they'd given away the last of the notes they gave each other high fives and then scuttled back into the hole in the wall.

'Mum shouted, "Wakey-wakey, daydreamer." As she yanked me onto the bus I looked over and noticed Big Issues' dog sticking his tongue out at me. As we drove by I saw it was a £50 note flapping between his teeth.

'Felix? Felix, come back!'

The Cat PM at No 10

A version of this poem was performed at No 10 Downing Street on 24th November 2015

There once was a cat at Number 10,
Who fancied himself as the PM.
He'd jump on the desk then sit in the chair
When the real Prime Minister wasn't there.

Purring as he licked his paws,
Meowing as he stretched his claws.
He imagined all the things he'd do
If all his policies came true.

Yes, Mr Cameron's a kind human
And so's his wife – the lovely Sam.
But from now on let's be very clear
About who really is the boss round here.

Once every feline has the vote,
No longer will George Osborne gloat.
All MP's would be de-selected
And only cats could be elected.

Cats in power! Cats in charge!
Cats at leisure! Cats at large!
Cats are smarter! Cats are cool!
Cats' Magna Carta – when Cats rule!

Those wretched cat flaps will be banned,
Proclaim the news throughout the land.
Wait at the door, we'll let you know
When we wish to come and go.

If it rains we want a feller,
To protect us with a big umbrella.
And should we choose to take a nap,
You must provide a nice warm lap.

And if we wish to use your garden,
We certainly will not beg your pardon.
We'll do our business where we choose,
Do not shoo us – don't abuse.

We'll shut you in the Albert Hall,
While ten cats' choirs caterwaul.
Then we'll hurl soil, sticks and stones
To make you hurtle to your homes.

Cats in power! Cats in charge!
Cats at leisure! Cats at large!
Cats are smarter! Cats are cool!
Cats' Magna Carta – when Cats rule!

Every dog will be our slave.
If any of them misbehave,
If they rebel, if they say no,
We'll send them to a firework show.

No birds shall taunt us from a tree,
The ground will be their territory.
We will so enjoy the slaughter
As fish must jump out of the water.

Every louse will be re-housed
And every house must have a mouse
And every flat must have a rat
And every cat must have a mat.

We intend to close our borders
To those who'll not obey our orders.
If you don't do as we please,
We will make you refugees.

All babies will be micro-chipped,
Macho males will have the snip.
Eventually to make more space,
We'll get rid of the human race.

Cats in power! Cats in charge!
Cats at leisure! Cats at large!
Cats are smarter! Cats are cool!
Cats' Magna Carta – when Cats rule!

NOBODY'S HOME

Annie hasn't anyone,
Owen's on his own.
Sally likes her solitude,
Alan lives alone.

Izzy lives in isolation,
So I shouldn't moan.
I may not meet a multitude
When entering my home,

But at least I live with Nobody
And Nobody lives with me.
We share the housework equally,
He keeps me company.

On the mornings I rise early,
He walks me to the door.
All day he waits so patiently,
My friend for evermore?

Solitary Snowdrop

I am a solitary snowdrop
On the mountainside.
On a slope, behind a rock
Is where I reside.

I don't know how I got here,
How this became my home.
I hope if I pop up next year,
I will not be alone.

Go Mild In The Country

*If you go down to the woods today you'll not get
a big surprise …*

The woodland is surrounded
By an electric fence.
Please keep on the pathway,
If you stray, it's an offence.

The trail is paved with tarmac,
The café's not too dear,
Or why not skip straight to the shop
And buy a souvenir?

The signs along the route
Will give you information
Of all the wild things that once thrived
Before our transformation.

Most trees have been replaced
By Forestry Officials
With safer stock that won't fall down
Because they're artificial.

As well as Woodland Wardens,
For your security,
Keeping watch like hawks above
Is our CCTV.

Nothing's lurking in the undergrowth,
You'll hear no rustling.
We've no flora nor no fauna
That do not quite fit in.

We don't have creepy crawlies,
No spiders are allowed.
The rooks and ravens were dismissed
Because they were too loud.

There are no poisonous berries,
The brambles have no thorns.
The nettles have been neutered
And the flowers have been warned

Not to splay their petals lewdly
To just any pollinator,
But to be discreet or they'll end up
In the incinerator.

We evicted all the woodlice
From their rotting log,
We've picked off all the fungus
And we've drained the stinking bog.

Ugly toads will not be found,
Nor will snakes or bats.
There's nothing for the squeamish here,
Certainly not rats.

We've purified the water,
The fish are in a tank.
The lake's no longer murky,
Now the ducks stay on the bank.

We've exterminated hornets,
Removed the stingers from the bees.
The wasps have been excluded,
And the ants are CRB'd.

Our wildlife has been vetted,
And so have all our staff.
From next year even customers
Must pass a polygraph.

The mosquitoes have got ASBOs,
The weasels have been tagged.
The polecats are in rehab
And the squirrels have been gagged.

Mice have all been poisoned,
Magpies are out on bail.
The minks have to be tasered,
And the moles are all in jail.

The fox perpetually terrorised
Our fluffy bunny rabbits,
So one morning, before opening,
Our marksman duly shot it.

There were run-ins with the badgers,
They simply ruined our landscaping.
So we gassed them in their tunnels
To stop them excavating.

We had so many deer
The woods were overrun.
We culled them so effectively,
Lucky you, if you spot one!

Cute and cuddly creatures
And those that will adhere
To our strict code of conduct
Are what you will find here.

We're cleaning up the countryside
For the common good.
Enjoy what's left before it's gone,
Welcome to our wood.

The Higgledy-Piggledy Hedge

Not last year but the year after that, there was a man who moved into the old cottage on the edge of the village. He had lived in the city all his life and liked hustle and bustle and things to do.

In the countryside time tick-tocks slowly but the man knew how to keep himself busy. One day he moved his bed from one side of the room to the other. On another, he swapped the front door with the back door. He took off the old roof and put on a new roof. He knocked down walls to make the rooms bigger and then built new walls to make the rooms smaller.

One afternoon he looked out of the window. His eyes followed the path to the bottom of the garden which led to something he didn't like the look of. Beside the old oak tree in the corner, there was a row of straggly trees and scruffy bushes cluttering up the place and making it look untidy. What on earth was it?

He phoned the farmer across the lane who told him that it was a higgledy-piggledy hedge. A higgledy-piggledy hedge? He didn't like the sound of that. He walked down the garden path to take a closer look.

Most of the creatures living in the higgledy-piggledy hedge were hiding by the time the man arrived. Only the flutterbies and bumbly bees flitted and buzzed about the purple and pink, the blue and the red, the yellow and white flowers swaying in the summer breeze. But the man didn't notice any of these, nor did he see the ladybird lazing on a leaf beneath his nose.

'A higgledy-piggledy hedge at the bottom of my garden? This won't do at all,' he said out loud.

'What's needed here is a nice new fence. A wall of wood, all stiff and straight and neat and tidy. That's what I want to see.'

The man went indoors to look at pictures of axes, saws and shredders in glossy catalogues. A big bonfire was something to look forward to. He imagined the blazing flames and the billowing smoke as the hedge crackled and burned. The thought of the smell of the smoke made him want a bacon sandwich and so he fried up some rashers and squashed them between two chunks of bread for his supper.

Meanwhile in the higgledy-piggledy hedge at the bottom of the garden, the ladybird told the flutterbies who told the wren, who told the slow worm who told the dormouse, who told the hedgehog who told the rabbit, who told the robin who told the old oak tree what the ladybird had heard.

'What!' growled the old oak tree. 'A nice new fence instead of a higgledy-piggledy hedge? You can't live on a wall of wood all stiff and straight and neat and tidy!'

'No we can't,' pipped the ladybird, 'the higgledy-piggledy hedge is our home.'

'No we can't,' spluttered the flutterbies, 'the higgledy-piggledy hedge keeps us warm in winter.'

'No we can't,' tweeted the wren, 'the higgledy-piggledy hedge is where I lay my eggs in spring.'

'No we can't,' squeaked the dormouse, 'the higgledy-piggledy hedge keeps me cool in the summer.'

'No we can't,' hissed the slow worm, 'I like to snuggle in autumn's fallen leaves.'

'No we can't,' barked the hedgehog, 'without the higgledy-piggledy hedge I'm just a hog.'

'N-n-no w-w-we c-c-can't,' stuttered the rabbit, 'I c-c-can't m-m-make a-a-a w-w-warren i-i-in a-a-a w-w-wall o-o-of w-w-wood.'

'No we can't,' chirped the robin, 'It's our larder where all the nuts and berries grow. How would *he* like to live on a nice new fence?'

'No you can't,' growled the old oak tree, 'a wall of wood, all stiff and straight and neat and tidy? That won't do at all. You can't live on a nice new fence!'

Sleep did not come easily for the man that night. Branches groaned and leaves rustled outside in the dark. It sounded as if the old oak tree was walking towards the house. 'Don't be silly,' he mumbled. But still, he pulled the covers over his head until at last, in the early hours of the morning, he drifted off.

But there was no rest in his dreams either. When he'd fallen asleep his bed had been soft and cosy, but now it felt hard and rough. He turned over and saw that his bed had changed into a wall of wood. He rubbed his eyes and saw that it was exactly what he wanted to build at the bottom of the garden. It was his nice new fence. A wall of wood, all stiff and straight and neat and tidy. And he was on top of it!

OOPS!

Not for long. He fell off with a

BUMP!

He climbed back up and tried to lie down on it again. But the top was so narrow he rolled over and fell off onto the other side.

BONK!

Oh, but he was so tired. He leaned against the fence and closed his eyes, but after a while that made his feet ache and his head dizzy.

He scrambled up the nice new fence again and tried to sleep with his body dangling down on either side, but this made his tummy sore.

Then he straddled it as if it was a skinny horse, but a cold wind blew from one side and hot air blasted from the other. Half of him was frozen and half of him was scorched.

The fence stretched ahead and behind him into the distance. 'Longer than the Great Wall of China,' he thought. And it was a dull brown colour. 'It's not very interesting,' he sighed.

As if that wasn't bad enough, there was nothing else to look at. No animals, no birds, no flowers, no trees. Just him and the nice new fence. Nothing to do but pull splinters out of his bottom.

And what was there to eat? He leant down and chomped a chunk out of one of the many millions of dull brown planks. It didn't taste too bad but the idea of eating wood for the rest of his life turned his tongue to sandpaper.

He was beginning to wish he'd never had the idea of putting up a nice new fence at the bottom of the garden when the fence began to

wiggle like a giant worm. He held on tightly as
it wriggled like an eel. Then it squiggled like a
snake and began to bounce up and down like a
bucking bronco.

WOAH!

He couldn't hold on any longer and was tossed
into the air ...

WHEEEEEEEEEEE!

... he landed with a

CRASH!

on his bedroom floor.

The man picked himself up and drew back the curtains.

The sun was shining on the old oak tree. The birds were singing and rabbits were scampering to and fro. Flutterbies and bumbly bees flitted and buzzed about the purple and pink, the blue and the red, the yellow and white flowers swaying in the summer breeze. A ladybird leapt from a leaf and flew off into the field beyond.

'A nice new fence might not be such a good idea after all,' said the man to himself, 'but that higgledy-piggledy hedge at the bottom of the garden could do with a trim and a tuck. I think I'll have a word with the farmer across the lane. Perhaps he'll give me some good advice and even help me tidy it up a bit, so then it could last forever and ever.'

Flora, Shut The Door-a!

'Flora, shut the door-a!
Please do not ignor-a
Our request, we know what's best,
The lecky bill will soar-a.'

She would not shut the door-a
Although we did implore her.
So snow swept in up to her chin,
Now Flora will not thaw-a.

Cosmic Barbecue

A shooting star fell in our pond,
We watched it as it crashed.
It flashed past the greenhouse
And then made quite a splash.

Frogs were frazzled, toads were toast,
The goldfish were aglow.
Dragonflies burst into flame
And scorched the grass below.

Owls and bats combusted,
Newts and gnats were nuked.
The fountain shot out fireworks,
Cats and dogs were spooked.

Dad could not put out the blaze,
Nor could the fire brigade.
Mum said, 'It's our lucky star,
There's money to be made.'

And ever since that meteorite,
There's always been a queue
For sizzling flame grilled grub cooked on
Our cosmic barbecue.

O Spotty, Up Yours!

Mum says I'm making a mountain out of a molehill,
But I say, 'O Spotty, Up Yours!'

There's a monkey on my shoulder,
It wears a tartan suit.
The checks are even louder
Than the monkey's trumpet's toots.

The elephant I'm sitting on
Has toe-nails painted red.
A tittle-tattling toucan
Is perched upon my head.

But *they're* not what you notice,
If it was I wouldn't care.
The thing that makes me sad is,
The sight that makes you stare.

For the only thing, the only thing,
The only thing you see,
Is the thing that hurts me like a sting,
The thing that upsets me, is ...

The Spot, the Spot, the Spot I've got,
The zit on the tip, like a lighthouse glows.
The Spot, the Spot, the Spot I've got,
The blot on the top of my nose.

It does not please me,
It does unease me,
It says please squeeze me,
Oh how you tease me.

Every day I hope it goes,
But every night it grows and grows.
It's red and angry, yellow-tipped,
I want to zap the little git.

I've got something I wish I'd not,
I just cannot forget-it-not,
It does not make me laugh a lot.

Why it picked me, goodness knows,
Why am I the one it chose?

The Spot, the Spot, the Spot I've got,
The zit on the tip like a rotten rose.
The Spot, the Spot, the Spot I've got,
The blot on the top of my nose.

Oh Spotty, you drive me dotty.
Scooter from my hooter!

Pizza Face

Louisa likes the pizza
From Luigi's place.
He puts the toppings on the cheeza
To look just like her face.

Exclamation Mark!

which witch?

Which witch was it
Who put a spell on me?
Who's turned me into something
I'm so surprised to be?

Which witch was it?
Was it Madgy Fidge,
Who turned the cheese and milk to black
When they were in the fridge?

Was it Muckleberry Mary
Who lives under the bridge?
She's only got one tooth and eye
And stinks of fish and cabbage.

You must know Molly Mable?
Her house is made of hay.
If a bug-a-boo is on your back
She'll make it go away.

Which witch was it
Who put a spell on me?
Who's turned me into something
I'm not supposed to be?

Was it the Ditch Witch?
Or the Stitch Witch?
Or the Snitch Witch?
Or the Kitsch Witch?
The Quitch Witch?
Or the Rich Witch?
Or the witch who lives
In Ipswich?

Witches live in Woolwich,
Norwich, Dulwich too.
Redditch, Greenwich, Magwitch,
There's one who lives by you.

Which witch was it?
I really want to know.
There's been a transformation,
To which witch should I go?

I've been turned into an ostrich,
I've got such strong long legs.
But I'm itching, so I'm scratching
And I've just laid an egg.

I sure don't want to crack it,
So to get rid of my fleas,
I need a lotion or some potion,
Oh won't you tell me, please?

So which witch was it
Who put a spell on me?
Who's turned me into a big bird?
I need a remedy.

Answer: It was Aunt Hagatha of course.

Suárez The Shark

Look who's dived in the swimming pool,
Fleeing from the land.
He used to kick a football,
But now he has been banned.

See that trail of bubbles,
Heading straight this way?
This will lead to trouble,
I don't think we should stay.

Get out quick before you're nipped
And your snorkel's smashed, your flippers ripped.
Fingers, toes – anything goes –
Ow! He's gripped my ears and bit my nose.

Suárez in the swimming pool,
Our bodies are now scarred.
The lifeguard blows her whistle,
Then shows him a red card.

Suárez the Shark has made his mark,
The water's stained with blood.

Clive PiG 83

Now he's running towards the park,
At loose in the neighbourhood.

The devil dogs have met their match,
So to these words please hark.
He won't let go – he won't detach –
His bite's worse than his bark.

He's getting more vicious day by day,
He's grown ferocious fangs.
Deadlier incisors than Dracula's,
He'll cull the local gangs.

If you're having a kick about,
Your game he'll come and spoil.
With gleaming evil needle teeth,
He'll bite and burst your ball.

So FIFA lift your nine match ban,
Clean up this blood sports' splatter.
I would be your greatest fan –
Yikes! He just ate that Sepp Blatter.

*Luis Suárez was banned for a biting incident
during the 2014 FIFA World Cup.*

Ukulele Ike On My One Wheeled Bike

I'm Ukulele Ike on my one wheeled bike,
Unicycling down the road.
I'm Ukulele Ike on my one wheeled bike,
Ukuleling as I go.

Some people take the train,
Some people catch the bus.
Some people take the plane,
But I don't like the fuss.

I prefer to take my time,
Although I do not stroll.
Upon my vehicle I climb
And down the hill I roll.

(Please do not impede my velocipede!)

I'm Ukulele Ike on my one wheeled bike,
Pedalling around the globe.
I'm Ukulele Ike on my one wheeled bike,
Travelling along the road.

Harmonicas in helicopters,
Dulcimers on double-deckers.
Caravanettes? Clarinets!
Magic carpets? Castanets!
Trombones on a tractor,
Oboes on an 'orse.
Gongs on a gondola,
I endorse all this of course.

(My mode of travel I've got sorted,
By my music I'm transported.)

I'm Ukulele Ike on my one wheeled bike,
Unicycling down the road.
I'm Ukulele Ike on my one wheeled bike,
Ukuleling as I go.

You might like to paraglide,
Or skateboard down the street.
Toboggan down a mountainside,
Or dance to a drum beat.
Walk upon a tightrope,
Pogo on a stick.
Canter on an antelope,
Or fly on a broomstick.

(I prefer to be conveyed in my own special way.)

I'm Ukulele Ike on my one wheeled bike,
Now I really have to go.
I'm Ukulele Ike on my one wheeled bike,
Time to wish you cheerio!

Whirly Girly

Sara Hurley got up early,
 Drank a pot of vinho verde.
  Then she played some Monteverdi
   On her auntie's hurdy-gurdy.
    Patterns on her dress
     Were swirly,
      And her teeth
       Were really pearly.
        Her aunt Shirley's
         Hair was curly,
          Burly brother Bran
           Was surly.
            Sara Hurley,
             Vinho verde,
              Monteverdi,
               Hurdy-gurdy,
                Swirly, twirly
                 Auntie Shirley,
                  Curly, pearly,
                   Bran and surly,
                    Hurly-burly, Sara Hurley,
                     Was a really whirly girly.

(And then she was sick.)

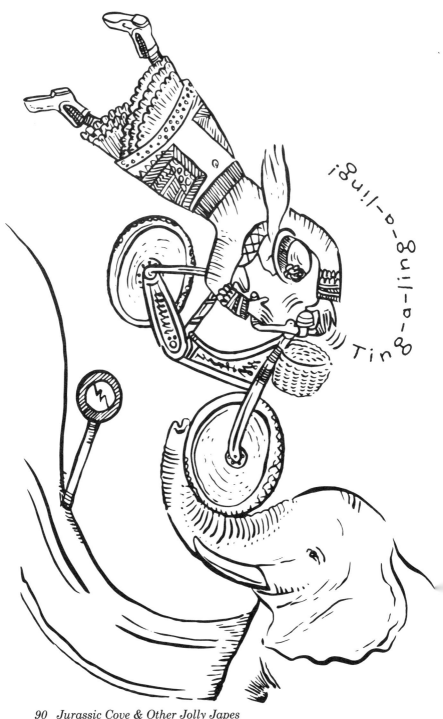

Is A Bell A Necessity?

Is a bell a necessity
When pedalling the highway?
Yes it is, especially
To shoo things out the way.

A yak on the track,
A crane in the lane.
Toads on the roads,
Parakeets in the streets.

Bulls in the boulevards,
Pheasants in the crescents.
Kangaroos in the avenues,
Manta rays on the motorways.

Ting-a-ling-a-ling!
Is all it takes
To warn them of one's presence.
An accident with an elephant
Is something quite unpleasant.

Paper Aeropain

Shane made a paper aeroplane
And chucked it in the sky,
But it shot straight down again
And stabbed him in the eye.

Wait in a queue in Kuwait?
In Kuwait that's what you do.
Huw waited with Kate
From 2 'til 8.
Their wait was so great
Their flight flew.

The Train To Turin

A man wakes up in the middle of the night in a foul mood. He turns to his wife who is snoring beside him and nudges her awake.

WIFE: What's up?
HUSBAND: It's all your fault!
W: What is?
H: That we got on the wrong train.

W: What train are you talking about?

H: The train in my dream.

W: Well, that's not my fault, because I wasn't in your dream.

H: Oh yes you were. We were on holiday in Italy waiting on the platform in Rome. I was buying a cappuccino when you shouted at me to hurry up because the train was arriving and you wanted to get a window seat. I grabbed the cup and then spilt hot coffee down the front of my brand new shirt as I rushed to get on the train.

W: Did I get one?

H: Of course not, you don't drink coffee.

W: No, you noodlehead! A window seat ... did I get a window seat?

H: Yes, *you* did, but *I* didn't. There were no seats left and I had to stand.

W: That's a pity.

H: You said the journey would only take half an hour but the train didn't stop at our station. You'd read the sign wrong. We were on the fast train to Turin and so I had to stand for the next two hours.

W: You see, if you hadn't queued for that coffee, we'd have been first on and you'd have been able to sit down. Anyway, it's all nonsense because I wasn't even in your dream last night.

H: Oh yes you were. You spent half the journey complaining about how difficult it would be to remove the brown stain on my shirt.

W: Show it to me then.

H: What?

W: The stain on your precious shirt.

H: All right. I'll get it from the laundry basket.

W: You shouldn't have left it in there!

H: Why not?

W: You should have soaked it in cold water straight away. It'll be hard to get the stain out now.

H: You could have told me that at the time!

W: How could I have told you? I wasn't even there.

H: Where were you then?

W: I can't remember.

H: That's because you nodded off after an hour on the train. You know what you're like when you first wake up. You're always in a bit of a daze.

W: That's because I'm such a deep sleeper.

H: Half the time you don't know where you are anyway.

W: Well, are we there yet?

H: Where?

W: Turin.

H: Of course we're not in Turin.

W: Well, why did you wake me up?

H: Because you were snoring and embarrassing us. All the other passengers were giving us funny looks.

W: Who cares about what other people think? I'm going back to sleep. Wake me up when we *do* get there.

And with that, she turned her back to her husband and went to sleep again. He got out of bed and rummaged through the laundry basket. He went downstairs to the kitchen and filled a bowl with cold water. Looking at the stain once more, he shook his head, raised his eyes to the ceiling and growled, 'It's all your fault!' Then he plunged the shirt into the water to soak.

Fly As A Kite

Me and Mum are on holiday in wet and windy Wales. Uncle Bobby's stayed at home because he stood on a rusty nail. Since the caravan was already paid for, we came anyway.

The caravan is covered in seagull splat. It has a flat tyre so when I'm in bed my feet are higher than my head. I wake up feeling dizzy. It's damp and musty and the kettle made a rattling sound the first time it boiled. When Mum poured the hot water on the tea bag a dead snail and a shrivelled brown slug came out of the spout.

This is the first day it hasn't bucketed down. I wanted to go to the seaside but Mum had picked up a leaflet from the service station about kite feeding in the hills. It took us two hours to get here and I sulked all the way.

I've never flown a kite. I didn't know they ate anything. I thought all they needed was a piece of string and a puff of wind. She said they are a type of hawk, like a buzzard, and are very rare.

Mum likes birds. She buys balls of fat and hangs 'em on the washing line in our yard. Uncle Bobby thinks that's stupid and a waste of money. Hc says in some countries people can't afford a ball of fat to feed their kids and what's the point of washing clothes if they end up stained with bird dunk. Mum says he's perfectly free to do his own laundry if he wishes. He wants to get a cat but he can't have one. Not while he's living in our house.

We're standing on a bit of land sticking out into the lake. There are tall trees all around the edges and behind them are loads of hills dotted with straggly sheep. I've counted twenty-two wind thingies standing like soldiers twirling rifles. They're grey, like the sky; grey, like the rocks; grey, like our car. Lots of people don't like them but if the blades were multi-coloured that might change their minds.

When I was in the infants we used to run around the playground whirling our arms round and round to see if we could take off like helicopters. Little Dickie wouldn't do it because he thought his hand would come off. Once I did it so fast, I couldn't stop and I whacked the new girl in the face and smashed her glasses.

Mum's legs are aching. She wants to sit down but the grass is wet. I spread a beach towel on the ground and she leans on me and I help her down.

Everyone seems excited but they're not talking much. Some of them have all the gear: weatherproofs, proper boots, big cameras and binoculars. They've got bags with flasks and sandwiches. Some have even brought their own chairs. They're the sort of people who leave the house expecting an emergency. They've probably stashed cans of WD40 in secret pockets in their cagoules. Most of them look like plonkers.

Not her though, the little girl with the yellow dress and freckles. Even though it's a dull afternoon she sparkles like a proper summer's day. I love her yellow hair sticking up like crazy. If she was a flower she'd be a buttercup. If I was a flower I'd be one of those smelly white ones you get on stinging nettles.

Who's she with? I can't see anyone. I bet she's called Oracle, or Sukey, or Florence. She's staring up at the sky with her wide eyes and her mouth open, waiting. Waiting, watching, like all the others.

Every day of the year they come here. Mum read the sign in the Visitor's Centre: 3 o'clock in the summer, 2 o'clock in the winter. Everyone's looking in the same direction.

I wonder if the King of the Kites says, 'If you've nothing better to do this afternoon why not flap off down to the lake? Watch the wingless two-legs hanging out. They're there every day – 3 o'clock in the summer, 2 o'clock in the winter – waiting and staring up at the sky.'

Mum said kites used to be common as rats and lived off rubbish in the streets. A long time ago you could be hanged if you killed a kite in London. But some people thought they were pests and found ways of getting rid of them. They were nearly extinct but now people want them back again. Perhaps that's what will happen to those wind machines. People who don't like them now will change their minds and then want more.

I wonder what they feed the kites on these days 'cos it's the seagulls that eat all the rubbish at our caravan site and I can't see any balls of fat hanging from washing lines here. If this was a horror movie we'd be their food – suddenly a tall fence would spring up from the ground and we'd be trapped and torn apart by ginormous birds of prey.

Mum spoke to the man standing beside us who was wearing a badge. He was short and hairy and his belly was even bigger than Uncle Bobby's. He said they're fed on bits of pork and beef. It's all good stuff, must be fit for human consumption. It costs eight grand a year, that's why you have to pay to get in. Then he nodded across the water and we saw a teenager with a red bucket come out from behind a bush and scatter scraps of meat on the grassy patch in front of giant Christmas trees.

I pull Mum to her feet. She's a lot heavier these days. But at least she's stopped smoking. Everyone is reaching for their binoculars and cameras like cowboys with six-shooters. Mum's checking the battery power in the video camera.

I see the first one. High up, on my left, coming from over the furthest hill. A dark shape blown by the wind, like a couple of sticks covered with rags. Then from out of nowhere, come three more. They hardly flap their wings at all. Just lazily glide, taking their time. They're not in a hurry for their grub. I hear Mr Big Belly say at this time of year, when harvesting is taking place, there's plenty of mice and voles for them to eat and we'll have to wait a bit longer before they come down and feed. He says what they're doing now is meeting up and hanging out, just the way we humans are doing down here. He thinks this is funny because he laughs. It sounds like a bear grunting.

Then one comes from out of the trees, close over our heads. Awesome! It's nutty red and massive. Its eyes and beak look wicked. Its wings are as wide as I can stretch my arms. It swoops low and in a slow straight line, as cool as a model on the catwalk, it skims across the water so the crowd can snap their cameras, and then it rises up and joins the others. There's thirty or more now, drifting in a blue sky and the sun's come out at last and the wind's easing and they're hanging in the air.

We're all staring up and no-one's talking. Everyone's looking at the kites with forked tails, at the kites with no strings. I feel tears in my eyes. I turn to Mum. She's switched off the camera and I can see she's been crying because her eyes are puffy and her face is shiny.

I put my arm around her. Mum's always said she'd like to see a blue whale before she dies but she knows she never will. Perhaps this will be good enough for her.

They're calling to each other, sending out strange sounds across the skies. It's a weird screeching and whistling noise. Like a cry of pain. I guess they're saying hello. Mind you, they probably see each other everyday. What have they got to talk about? Us down below? The lazy wind catchers on a go-slow? The awful summer we've been having? Who knows?

Then there's another sound, *crak crak,* a big black bird – mum says it's a raven – has flown down to the grass bank and is stabbing at pieces of meat with its beak. This gets the kites going. Here they come. One, two, three, down they drop but don't touch the ground. There's more – four, five, six – they pick up scraps with their claws and fly off again. Ten, twenty, thirty, again and again, they rain down and wave their wings as if dancing, grabbing the food with their claws and then rise up and drop down for more. Dive-bombing acrobats. It's amazing. Now it really does seem as if they've got strings attached. How can they zoom down so fast without crashing into the ground and then pull themselves back up so quickly? They're so big, but then, they must also be so light. Wow!

Then I see the little girl in the yellow dress. She's on the side of the lake where the kites are feeding. She's skipping and spinning and flapping her arms, pretending to be a bird. Next, she jumps and squats down and pecks a piece of meat into her mouth and pretends to fly up. She swallows the food and then squats down for more.

No-one is moving. The wind has dropped. All eyes are on the girl.

She hops towards the lake and kneels at the edge. With her arms behind her she darts her face in and out of the water taking quick, short sips. Then she looks up and calls to the sky in a high pitched voice, *'pew, pew, pew, pew.'*

A cloud blots the sun. Mum gasps and points up. Above us the sky is full of kites. Hundreds of them, hanging in the air. Waiting, watching, waiting.

'Pew, pew, pew, pew,' the girl calls again.

Cameras are clicking like crazy and the sky fills with the kites' answering cries.

'Pew, pew, pew, pew, click-click-click-click, pew, pew, pew, pew.'

What with the lake being surrounded by trees and hills we're in a huge bowl of sound.

Now the girl is simply standing like when I first saw her on this side of the lake, her mouth open and her eyes wide, looking up to the sky.

And then they come. People scream and hurtle by us. But me and Mum stay put. She holds my hand as the kites dive down and swarm around the girl. We watch them grip her by her hair, her clothes and skin and they lift her into the air and then the King of the Kites swoops beneath her and she stands on his back and is taken high over the tree line. She's smiling and talking to the birds close to her. Her arms are raised above her head and her wrists are gripped by two birds above her.

As her yellow hair and smiling freckles pass overhead, Mum says quietly,

'She looks as happy as a buttercup.'

The wind picks up as they fly from the lake over the trees, and the whirr of the wind thingies drowns the calls of the kites and the girl, as together, they soar out of sight beyond the hills.

Jewels That Spring From Underground

I like to think that when I've gone,
Something will remain
Of what I did upon this earth,
Though few will know my name.

And so it's time to let you know
Of one thing I have done.
If I don't tell you, no-one will,
And so, my dear grandson,

Did you know that long ago
Along the route we tread,
This used to be a railway track?
Now it's a cycle path instead.

Those orange flowers blooming
On the verges and the bank,
Did not pop up all on their own
It's me you've got to thank.

I scattered seeds there just last year,
Like confetti at a wedding.
And so for summers evermore,
There'll be this pretty bedding.

For the marigolds bring happiness
To bees and butterflies,
Jewels that spring from underground
Will catch the eye of passers-by.

I don't have much to leave you,
So think of these as treasure.
Money cannot buy you love,
But flowers are pure pleasure.

Granny sang me a lullaby
When I lay in her bed.

While I sucked a minty
She'd caress my head.

Her cardie smelt of moth balls
And I remember too

She kept some sprigs of lavender
Hanging in the loo.

Wave Farewell

We took his ashes to the beach
With our buckets and spades
And we sculpted his body out of sand
And we made
A replica of him
That was even better looking.

He'd have been pleased,
Then Penelope sneezed
As we sprinkled the ashes
From his head to his toes
A gust of wind blew
Dust of him up her nose.
Some laughed, some cried
As we do every day
Since Cornelius died.

When you passed away
I was holding your hand,
Now the one I stroke is made of sand.
Soon waves will wash you from the land
But before they do you'll lie in the sun
And we play volleyball

And when that's done
We sit around you
And we talk about you
And learn more about you.

Beneath seagulls' sighs
You've got shells for eyes
And a seaweed beard
People passing by probably think we're weird
And then a dog – stupid dog –!
Scampers over you
And your feet have crumbled before they're due,
But it's not a problem to bring them back
We've made you once, we've got the knack.

And it's just in time
For the tide's coming in,
It's time to stand
And watch the waves roll up the sand.
They're coming to get you
To tickle your feet
You always loved me doing that.

The last time I came to your flat
You put two sugars in my tea

And as you stirred
You said to me,
Think sweet thoughts when you think of me.
Think of me as sugar
Dissolving in the sea.

And I do, as you're slowly washed away,
I do as you're gently washed away.
The sea licks you just like my cat
Licks me, when sitting on my lap
As you're washed away,
                washed away.

The sea licks you like my cat
When sitting, purring on my lap
As you're washed away,
                washed away,
                        washed away...

The End Of The Line

A poem doesn't have to rhyme
All the time
It's fine.

It's not a crime
And not a bad sign
If it doesn't rhyme
Each or every other line.

This one doesn't
Does it?

Going, Going, Gone

They're not going
So she's not going
And he's not going
And you're not going
And *I'm* not going!

They *are* going
But she's not going
So hc's not going
And you're not going
And *I'm* not going!

They are going
And *she* is going
But he's not going
So you're not going
And *I'm* not going!

They are going
And she is going
So *he* is going
But you're not going
And *I'm* not going!

They are going
And she is going
And he is going
So *you* are going
Well, *I'm* not going!

They are going
She is going
He is going
You are going
And *I* am going!

Where are we going?
We're all going to ...   .

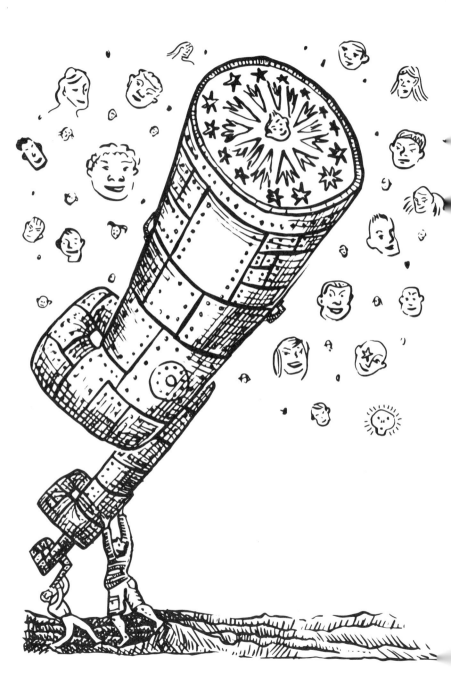

As Many Stories As Stars?

One summer's night on the beach by a cave, a father and son are sitting by the campfire. The young boy asks,

'Are there really as many stories as stars?'

The man thinks for a while and then shakes his head and says,

'No, there are many, many more stories than stars. For every star has a story, and every planet has a story, and every moon has a story, and every mountain, every river, every sea has a story, and every fish, every bird, every tree has a story, and every house, every village, every city has a story, and every child, every woman, every man has a story.'

Then he threw another log on the fire and showers of sparks fizzed.

And he began another story ...

"I love this book!"
★★★★★
Ewan Mee

£5.99 + p&p
clivepig.co.uk

Clive PiG's first book.

PiG's Tales is a compendium of Clive's choicest cuts including *Colin the Chocolate Kid, Nice is Nasty, Suzanne Loved a Snowman, Our Dad's Not Normal* and *The Angry Dormouse*.

"Clive's book is fabulous and was so well received by our students we've sold out. Please send more books now!" – **Leanne Magee, Primary Literacy Co-ordinator, St Andrews International School, Bangkok. Book Week 2016**

Published by Caboodle Books Ltd
ISBN 978-0-9569482-3-6